BY VALERIE SCHO CAREY

ILLUSTRATED BY DIRK ZIMMER

A Laura Geringer Book

An Imprint of HarperCollins*Publishers*

Tsugele's Broom
Text copyright © 1993 by Valerie Scho Carey
Illustrations copyright © 1993 by Dirk Zimmer

Library of Congress Cataloging-in-Publication Data
Carey, Valerie Scho.
  Tsugele's broom / by Valerie Scho Carey ; illustrated by Dirk Zimmer.
     p.   cm.
  "A Laura Geringer book."
  Summary: Despite the urgings of her well-meaning parents, a self-
sufficient girl insists she'll never marry unless she meets
a man who is as reliable as her broom.
  ISBN 0-06-020986-0.—ISBN 0-06-020987-9 (lib. bdg.)
  [1. Brooms and brushes—Fiction.   2. Poland—Fiction.]
I. Zimmer, Dirk, ill.   II. Title.
PZ7.C21434Ts   1993   92-9873
[E]—dc20   CIP
                                                        AC

For my parents, Zelda Markowitz Scho and Ira Cass Scho, for the love they gave each other and the love they gave to us.

V.S.C.

To Willa Alma
D.Z.

NOT SO LONG AGO, in the village of Potsk, there lived a girl by the name of Tsugele. Tsugele was her parents' treasure. She washed the family's clothes, fed the chickens, swept the floor, baked the challah, and did the shopping. Her parents were certain that one day she would make a perfect wife and mother. "The man who marries our Tsugele," they were fond of saying, "will be a lucky man indeed."

One day Tsugele's parents called her before them.

"It is time you were married," said her mother.

"We will go to the matchmaker and see what she can do," said her father.

Tsugele laid her broom against a chair.

"No," she said.

"No?" said her father, taking a step backward and catching one foot in Tsugele's scrubbing pail.

"No?" said her mother, her hand flying to her mouth.

"No," repeated Tsugele calmly. "With my broom, I sweep floors. With my broom, I chase cats out of the chimney in the winter. With my broom, I beat rugs clean and brush ashes from the bake oven. Find me a man as reliable as my broom and I will marry him. Till then I see no reason why a strong and clever girl should marry."

"Nonsense!" shouted her father. "Every girl needs a husband."

"Not really," said Tsugele.

"But every girl *wants* a husband," protested her mother.

"Not me," said Tsugele.

"Tomorrow we visit the matchmaker," said her father firmly.

"She'll find you a good husband," said her mother.

"We'll see," said Tsugele.

But no one heard her.

A few days passed. The matchmaker sent a suitor to call on Tsugele.

The young man stood in the doorway turning his profile so that the light struck what he considered his "best side."

Tsugele looked up from the table where she stood polishing a large brass pot. "Won't you stay for dinner?" she asked.

"Of course," said the young man, gazing at his image in the pot.

"If you fetch me some water from the well, I'll prepare a soup for our meal," said Tsugele.

The young man scowled. "Work calluses my hands," he complained.

"Work or go hungry," answered Tsugele.

So the young man headed for the well. But when he leaned over to lower the bucket into the water, he caught sight of his reflection. "Ah, so handsome," he exclaimed. And there he sat admiring himself for the rest of the afternoon.

When at last he returned to the house, it was getting dark. He arrived to find Tsugele clearing away the dinner dishes.

"I'm sorry, but we've already had our dinner," she said.

So the young man left, muttering darkly.

"Don't worry," said the matchmaker when she learned what had happened. "That one is not the only straw in the broom."

The next day a new suitor came to call.

"Greetings!" he announced, and bowed gracefully. "I have heard you're a hardworking girl with a heart of pure gold. But no one told me to expect a beauty too!"

"And you, sir," said Tsugele, studying the man's shabby coat and poorly patched pants, "are quick with words. Are you as quick with your wits?"

When the man was seated comfortably at the table with a cup of tea, Tsugele set before him a butter churn and a large basket of washing.

"I'll go to market to buy what we need for dinner if you'll churn the butter and do the wash while I'm gone," she said.

"No trouble at all!" said the suitor.

So Tsugele took up her basket and shawl and left the house.

The man scratched his jaw and thought. "What is the quickest way to get this done with the least bother?" A moment later he was scurrying about collecting ropes and nails, hammers and saws, wood and a wagon wheel. Then he set to work pounding and sawing. "Now for the power to run this fine machine," he said when he had finished. And he strode outside. Soon he returned with a cat under one arm and a dog tied to a rope. He fastened the two to the strange contraption and watched them take off. Round and round they went as the gears and cranks pumped the churn up and down, up and down. "That is that," he said, smiling broadly. "Soon Tsugele will have all the butter she needs." Then he picked up the dirty laundry and a length of rope and went out again.

He walked straight to the river and strung the laundry in the water. "Why waste my time when the river can wash everything clean?" And so the happy man made himself comfortable beneath a tree and fell sound asleep.

Before long, a goat wandered by and began nibbling at the rope. He chewed until the clothing spilled into the rushing river.

When at last the man awoke, everything was gone.

"Ai ai ai!" he wailed, and he ran back to the house. He pushed open the door. There was the churn, lying on its side. The floor was awash in milk. Flecks of cream sprayed the air as the cat and dog raced round and round after each other. What a mess!

When the man saw what he had done, he turned and fled without looking back.

That night, Tsugele spoke to her parents. "I don't want to meet any more suitors," she said. "I want to go out into the world."

Her mother turned pale and nearly fainted. Her father gasped and choked on his bread. "No!" he shouted, knocking the tea from the table. But in the end they gave in, for they loved their daughter and could not bear to see her unhappy.

The next day, Tsugele packed her bag and took her broom in her hand. She kissed her parents good-bye and set off into the world.

Arriving at a neighboring town, she learned that Mendel the Merchant and his wife were looking for a housekeeper.

"I'm Tsugele from Potsk, and I'm a good worker," she told them.

"I'm Mendel," said the little man with the great, round belly.

"Can you cook?" asked Mendel's wife, who was just as plump as he.

"Yes, indeed!" said Tsugele.

"Then you're hired," said Mendel.

Tsugele worked hard and was happy at Mendel the Merchant's house. But Mendel and his wife worried about her.

"She's a good girl," said the wife.

"But a lonely one," said Mendel. "I hate to see anyone lonely."

"We must do something," said his wife. "We must arrange a match for her."

"I know just the fellow for Tsugele," said Mendel. "Yankle the Leather Goods Man! With him she'll lead a good life."

But when Mendel told Tsugele of his plan to introduce her to his friend, she was angry.

"I can do very well taking care of myself, thank you," she said, and went off in a huff.

That night Tsugele dreamed she was sweeping the floor. As she swept, the floor grew larger and larger. The room filled with people, all smiling at Tsugele. Her plain smock suddenly turned into a lovely dress—a bride's dress with a crown of flowers and a veil! And the broom in her hands changed into a man! The two of them danced together, whirling and sweeping across the floor.

Tsugele could see her partner clearly. He was lean and spare, and he stood very straight. His wiry hair was the color of straw. It would not lie flat, but stuck out from his head at odd angles. His hands were thin and rough like the wood of her broom handle. But his eyes were gentle when he looked at her.

The wedding guests formed a circle around the couple and began to clap their hands and stamp their feet in time to the music. The noise grew louder and louder. Finally it woke her.

Tsugele sat up. She rubbed her eyes, washed and dressed hurriedly, ate a quick breakfast, and went for her broom to start the day's cleaning. But the broom was not in its usual corner. Nor was it by the stove, nor under the bed, nor anyplace else in her room.

"Perhaps I left it on the porch," Tsugele said to herself. But the broom was not there either.

Tsugele sat down on the steps. She was trying to remember where her broom might be when the sound of chopping made her look up. She was surprised to see a stranger at the woodpile. "You there!" she called to the man with the ax. "Who are you?" The sun shone brightly, and Tsugele had to shield her eyes. The stranger's hair was the color of straw and stood out stiffly from his head. Tsugele went closer. "Perhaps he's a beggar out to steal firewood," she thought. "Oh, I wish I had my broom. I would give him such a thrashing."

"You there!" she called again. "What's your name?" But no answer came, as the man went on working.

At last, when she stood directly in front of him, the stranger looked up and smiled.

Tsugele had the oddest feeling that she knew him. "Excuse me, sir," she stammered, "are you Mendel's new helper?"

The man said nothing. It was clear he was not used to talking much. Tsugele felt foolish. She tried to think of something else to say, but all that came out was "Have you seen my broom?"

"Yes, Tsugele" came the answer.

Tsugele blinked in surprise.

"Have we met before?" she asked cautiously. "I took you for a stranger, but you know my name."

"Oh, I'm no stranger," said the man, shaking his head. "Not to you, Tsugele." He laid down his ax and stood up straight, his arms folded across his chest. "My name is Broom."

Tsugele caught her breath. She began to giggle. "Broom! Excuse me, but that's a silly name."

"Of course it is," he answered, "but it's what you've always called me." And he laughed.

Tsugele liked the sound of his laughter and his voice. They were soothing sounds, like the *woosh, woosh* of her broom sweeping across a floor.

"Yes, I *do* know you," said Tsugele. She was a wise girl, who had been taught not to deny miracles, not even miracles that might take place in Mendel the Merchant's yard and to a girl from Potsk. "If eggs become chickens, and peach stones become trees, why couldn't a broom, God willing, become a man?" she said.

At that they both laughed.

"Will you marry me?" asked Broom.

"Yes," said Tsugele.

And they put their arms around each other and danced about the yard, raising a cloud of dust in the bright morning sun.